D1576191

The
Cow That Got
Her Wish

Modern Curriculum Press
BEGINNING
TO
READ
Series

The
Cow That Got
Her Wish

Margaret Hillert

Illustrated by Krystyna Stasiak

ISBN: 0-8136-5621-4
Printed in the United States of America

22 23 24 25   06

1-800-321-3106
www.pearsonlearning.com

"I want to have fun,"
said Brownie, the cow.
"I want to have fun—
and I think I know how.

"There once was a cow
that jumped over the moon.
That's what I want to do,
and I'll start right at noon."

"Why, I can't play the fiddle.
I can't play a tune.
And a silly old cow
can't jump over the moon."

7

"Oh, no," said her friends.
"If you try such a jump,
do you know what will happen?
You're sure to go BUMP.

"And besides," they all said,
" you can't do it at noon!
Way up in the sky
you can't see any moon."

The cow was not happy.
She ate and she sat.
She sat and she ate
and she waited and sat.

"I'll wait till the sun sets,
and then very soon,
I know I'll be up, up,
and over the moon.

11

"I will go for a walk.

"I will climb up a hill
and jump over the moon.
Yes, I will. Yes, I will.

"I think I can make it.
Just look at me jump.
One, two, three. Here I go.
I go up, up, and —

15

BUMP!"

17

"Now, look," said her friends.
"Here's a lump and a hump.
What a silly old Brownie
to think you can jump."

"But I want to, I want to,
I want to, I say.
I know I can do it.
I'll find a good way.

"I'm tired," said Brownie.
"I sit and I sit.
I never have fun.
Not a bit. Not a bit.

"I know what I'll do.
I will try a balloon.
I'm sure that will help me
jump over the moon.

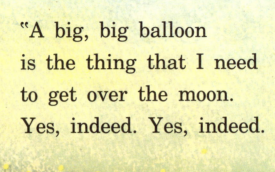

"A big, big balloon
is the thing that I need
to get over the moon.
Yes, indeed. Yes, indeed.

"Up, up, I will go now.
Up, up, I will jump.
This balloon is a help.
Here I go. Here I —

BUMP!"

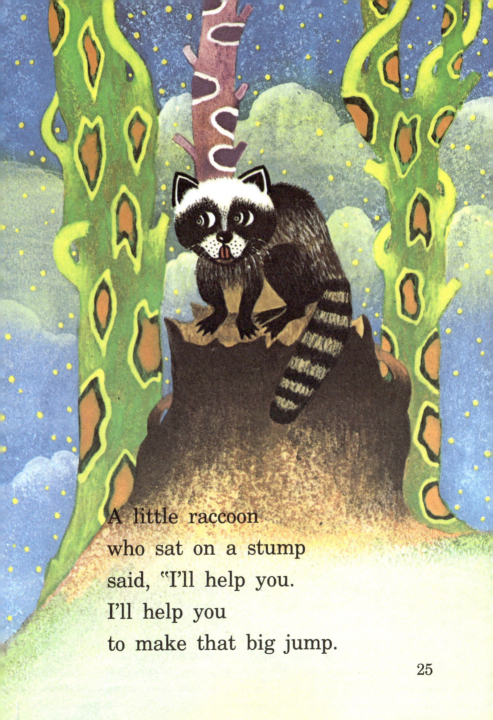

A little raccoon
who sat on a stump
said, "I'll help you.
I'll help you
to make that big jump.

25

"Just look over here.
Do you see what I see?
Here's the moon
round and yellow
and big as can be.

"If you take a big run,
if you make a big jump,
you'll go over the moon,
and you will not go BUMP."

27

So the brown and white cow
took a run and a jump.
And she made it! She made it
without any BUMP.

29

"I did it!
I did it!
Oh, thank you, Raccoon,
for now I'm the cow
that jumped over the moon."

31

Margaret Hillert, author and poet, has written many books for young readers. She is a former first-grade teacher and lives in Birmingham, Michigan.

In addition to giving practice with words that most children will recognize, *The Cow That Got Her Wish* uses the 13 enrichment words listed below.

besides	indeed	once	tune
climb	moon	raccoon	waited
		round	
fiddle	noon		
		stump	
happen			